KT-559-450

# Shh!
## WE HAVE A PLAN

### CHRIS HAUGHTON

30131 05347357 2

LONDON BOROUGH OF BARNET

Peace cannot be kept
by force; it can only be
achieved by understanding.

Albert Einstein

**To my youngest sister Lynn**

First published 2014 by Walker Books Ltd
87 Vauxhall Walk, London SE11 5HJ

This edition published 2015

10 9 8 7 6 5 4 3 2 1

© 2014 Chris Haughton

The right of Chris Haughton to be identified as
author/illustrator of this work has been asserted by him
in accordance with the Copyright, Designs and Patents Act 1988

This book has been typeset in SHH

Printed in China

All rights reserved. No part of this book may be reproduced,
transmitted or stored in an information retrieval system in
any form or by any means, graphic, electronic or mechanical,
including photocopying, taping and recording, without prior
written permission from the publisher.

British Library Cataloguing in Publication Data: a catalogue
record for this book is available from the British Library

ISBN 978-1-4063-6003-5

www.walker.co.uk

WALKER BOOKS
AND SUBSIDIARIES

LONDON · BOSTON · SYDNEY · AUCKLAND

MIX
Paper from
responsible sources
FSC
www.fsc.org
FSC® C104723

hello
birdy

shh         SHH!         we have a plan

ready one

ready two          ready three ...

LOOK!
up there

ready
one

ready
two

ready
three ...

LOOK!
down there

hello birdy

would you like
some bread?

one

two

three

ready one          ready two?

ready th...

RUN AWAY!

SHH! we have a plan